• Henry Holt and Company • New York

SQUARE FISH

MAMA CAT
has three kittens

Denise Fleming

Mama Cat has three kittens,

Fluffy, Skinny, and Boris.

When Mama Cat
washes her paws,

Fluffy and Skinny wash their paws.

Boris naps.

When Mama Cat walks
the stone wall,

Fluffy and Skinny walk the stone wall.

Boris naps.

When Mama Cat
sharpens her claws,

**Fluffy and Skinny
sharpen their claws.**

Boris naps.

When Mama Cat
chases leaves,

Fluffy and Skinny
chase leaves.

Boris naps.

When Mama Cat digs in the sand,

Fluffy and Skinny dig
in the sand.

Boris naps.

When Mama Cat
curls up to nap,

Fluffy and Skinny

curl up to nap.

Boris stretches,
yawns,

washes his paws,

and **pounces**

on Fluffy, Skinny,
and Mama Cat.

Then Boris naps.

For Abigail, my first cat

Imprints of Macmillan
175 Fifth Avenue, New York, NY 10010
mackids.com

MAMA CAT HAS THREE KITTENS.
Copyright © 1998 by Denise Fleming. All rights reserved.
Printed in China by RR Donnelley Asia Printing Solutions Ltd.,
Dongguan City, Guangdong Province.

Henry Holt® is a registered trademark of Henry Holt and Company, LLC.
Publishers since 1866.
Square Fish and the Square Fish logo are trademarks of Macmillan and are
used by Henry Holt and Company under license from Macmillan.

Originally published in the United States by Henry Holt and Company
First Square Fish Edition: March 2013
Square Fish logo designed by Filomena Tuosto

Library of Congress Cataloging-in-Publication Data
Fleming, Denise.
Mama cat has three kittens / Denise Fleming.
Summary: While two kittens copy everything their mother does, their brother naps.
[1. Cats—Fiction. 2. Animals—Infancy—Fiction.] I. Title.
PZ7.F5994Mam 1998   [E]—dc21   98-12249

ISBN 978-0-8050-5745-4 (Henry Holt hardcover)
20 19 18 17 16 15 14

ISBN 978-0-8050-7162-7 (Square Fish paperback)
20 19 18 17 16

AR: 1.6 / LEXILE: AD360L

The artist used colored cotton rag fiber poured through hand-cut stencils to create the illustrations for this book.